Them

by

Lee Weatherly

First published in 2006 in Great Britain by
Barrington Stoke Ltd
www.barringtonstoke.co.uk

ISBN 1-842993-64-X

Printed in Great Britain by Bell & Bain Ltd

A Note from the Author

THEM is based on a true story.

When I was 13, there was a boy in our class called Carl who I really wanted to impress. Carl had this idea. I would pretend to "hear voices", then I would tell another boy called Brennan all about these 'voices' and get him really scared. I went along with Carl's idea. It meant he was my friend, and it seemed like a laugh.

But it wasn't funny for Brennan. He thought I was going mad and he was really worried about me. Was I going to be OK? And all the time, Carl and I were laughing at him behind his back.

When we told Brennan that it was all a joke, he was furious. He never spoke to me again. He never forgave me. I can't really blame him. I never forgot what we did to Brennan. After a long time, I thought I'd write a story about it.

How far would you go to get in with someone? Kylie and Jaz, the two girls in THEM, take their game a lot further than Carl and I took ours ... Can there be a happy ending?

I hope you enjoy THEM.

For Brennan

Contents

Chapter 1
Home Sweet Home

"Put those boxes in the kitchen, please," Mum said to the removal men. Then, as they stacked the boxes next to the fridge, she turned to me. Her face looked tense. "Kylie, you could help, instead of just standing around."

She didn't say *This is all your fault anyway*. But I knew that was what she was thinking.

I felt as if I might cry, but I shrugged as if I wasn't bothered. "What? D'you want me to start moving boxes around or something?"

"*No*, but you could start unpacking them!" Mum walked out of the open front door of the flat, and I heard her shout down the stairs. "Could you be careful with that, please?"

I shook my brown hair out of its ponytail, then pulled it back up again. I looked around me. Our new flat was full of dark, gloomy bits of furniture. The landlord had filled it with stuff that no-one else wanted. But the walls had just been painted. That was the only bright thing about the rooms.

My little sister Gemma was messing about in the back of the flat somewhere. Now she came into the lounge. She was holding a Barbie that had a pink skirt on and nothing else. Gemma looked sulky. "I hate it here," she said and thumped Barbie onto the sofa. "It smells."

It did, too. The flat smelled of damp and old cat pee. I started to say something nice, but suddenly Gemma screwed her face up and threw the Barbie at me, as hard as she could.

"I hate you!" she cried. "We would never have had to move here if it wasn't for you!" She ran into one of the bedrooms and banged the door shut after her.

Mum came in again. She looked annoyed. "Kylie, what—"

"Nothing! I'm going for a walk." I shoved past one of the removal men and ran down the stairs.

I slowed down once I got outside. Was it my fault that we had to leave our house and come and live in a flat in town? I thought about how Dan had shouted at me, how he had shoved his face up next to mine so that I could smell the whisky on his breath and feel flecks of his spit hitting my cheeks. I shivered at the thought of him, even though it was September, and still warm.

Alongside our block of flats was a narrow footpath. It was muddy and overgrown. I kicked a beer can out of my way as I walked down it. I came round the corner and saw the path led to some allotments.

I stared at the patchwork of small gardens and began to feel a bit better. It was the only bit of green I had seen since we left home to go to the shelter six weeks ago. That was before we came here. There hadn't been anything green at the shelter. It had been awful there, even if they had tried to make it all cheery and welcoming. The gate into the allotments was locked. I shook it, and it rattled. Should I climb over it? I looked around. There was no-one about.

A moment later I was over the gate and walking around the allotments. I breathed in deeply, drinking in the smell of plants and earth. After a bit, I sat down on an old wooden bench and pulled my legs up under me.

There were so many new things in my life that I didn't want to think about. Like our new flat, which wasn't new but old and grotty. And the new term at school, which started tomorrow. I felt sick when I thought about it. My old school had been bad enough – what would this one be like? It had looked awful when Mum drove me past it yesterday, like a prison camp.

I heard a clinking sound, and I span round. Someone was unlocking the gate! A few seconds later, a boy with fair hair and glasses walked in. He was carrying a big fork and a bucket. He stopped when he saw me.

"Who are you? You don't have an allotment here."

I stood up and wiped my hands on my jeans. "Um – I'm Kylie. I was just looking around."

The boy kept staring. *What a geek!* What was he looking at? "Look, I'll just go," I said and I started to move past him. He put out a hand to stop me.

"No, wait – I was just asking, that's all. My name's Adam." He held out his hand. It was long and thin, like the rest of him.

His face was covered in spots, half of them about to burst. I shook his hand slowly and wished I'd never come in here. "Hi. Um, maybe I should go now ..."

"Are you new here?" Adam said and he pushed his glasses straight with a finger.

I gave a sigh. OK, I was going to have to talk to him. "Yeah, we just moved in." I pointed to our block of flats, and he grinned.

"Really? Those are my flats, too. I live there with my mum."

Oh, great. "Yeah, brilliant. Well—"

"Do you want to help me weed my mum's allotment?" Adam asked. He swung his fork to and fro. "Come on, it's easy. See, these are the weeds." He walked over to one of the square patches of garden and knelt down.

He didn't look up to see if I'd followed. Somehow I found myself walking over to him. "I don't really like gardening," I said.

The sun glinted off his glasses as he peered up at me. "What were you doing in here, then?"

I shrugged. I didn't feel like telling him anything. Suddenly I had an idea. "Oh, I don't know. The voices in my head told me to come. I always do what the voices in my head tell me," I said.

Adam looked hard at me. I could see he was worried.

"That was a *joke*," I told him.

"Oh." He blinked. "Sure, I knew that."

I bet he didn't have any friends at all. Which meant that we might have a lot in common, if this school was as bad as my last one. I knelt down on the ground and pulled at a weed. I yanked it out hard and it came up, with lots of earth on its roots.

"I'm not really into gardening, either," said Adam after a moment. "I'm a scientist."

A scientist, right. He was *my* age. "Really?" I said.

He nodded. "Yeah, I love science. In fact, I've just made a water clock that can tell the time to the nearest ten minutes. I did it all myself. I had the idea of trying to make the water run more slowly and ..."

He went on and on about his stupid water clock. "What do you do for fun?" I asked. I stood up and brushed the earth off my jeans. "Or do you just do science all day?"

Adam bent down to pull up some weeds. "No, I do lots of things for fun," he said. "Like, I read loads of science fiction."

I tried not to laugh. "Science fiction, huh? I better go now," I said and I headed for the gate before Adam could stop me again.

As I pushed it open, he shouted after me, "It was nice meeting you!"

God, what an idiot!

Mum was outside on the road when I got back. She was holding Gemma by the hand. Her face was red and she looked fed up. "Where *were* you?" she asked.

"Nowhere," I told her. I hoped my jeans weren't all covered in earth.

Gemma stuck her tongue out at me. *I hate you*, she mouthed without making a sound.

****

That night I lay awake for hours in the tiny room I had to share with Gemma. I listened to her slow breathing, and the sound of traffic rumbling past. A street light shone just outside our window. It gave the room an orange glow. Everything felt so odd, so new.

In the end, I got up and opened one of the boxes I hadn't had time to unpack. Edward lay there, looking up at me – the old, old teddy bear that my dad had given me when I was just a baby. My *real* dad, I mean. Not Dan.

I took him out, and crawled back into my bed. I know it's babyish, but sometimes when I'm upset or can't sleep, it helps to have Edward with me. I can hardly remember my dad, but when I hold Edward, it's almost like he comes back to me. I put my arms round the bear's furry middle and gave a long sigh.

I fell asleep as I was cuddling him. It was as if I could still smell my dad as I hugged Edward's worn fur.

Chapter 2
Getting in with Jaz

From the second I walked into Bankside Secondary School the next day, I could see who was in charge of Year Nine – Jaz Parbinder. She had a sly, smug smile and masses of black hair. The brown school uniform looked great on her, like a fashion statement.

At break I stood and watched Jaz and her group. But I didn't want them to see. I had already made up my mind that I was never going to go through the same sort of crap that I had gone through at my last school, not

ever. Being tripped up in the corridors.
Finding my books ripped up in my locker.
Everyone laughing at me.

And that meant I had to be friends with
Jaz.

But there were loads of people ahead of
me in the queue to be Jaz's friend.
Everywhere she went she had a gang of
people all round her, boys and girls both.
Everyone waited to hear whatever she said
and laughed when she laughed.

"Jaz, look, have you seen this dress?" A
girl with red hair showed Jaz something in a
magazine.

Jaz gave her a look full of pity. "God, Izzy,
no-one would actually *wear* that. Look at the
stupid frills on it." Everyone sniggered. Izzy
looked like she wanted to sink into the
ground. She put the magazine back into her
bag.

13

My heart beat faster as I stepped closer to the group. Jaz didn't notice me. I tried so hard to think of something I could say to her. I wanted to say something witty and cool that would make her black eyebrows fly up with respect. I couldn't think of anything. And saying the *wrong* thing would be worse than saying nothing at all.

"Hi, Kylie." Suddenly Adam was standing there with a big grin on his face. He was in Year Nine too, *of course.*

Damn! I gave a weak smile. "Oh. Hi," I muttered.

"I've got a book for you." Adam waved a book at me. It had a spaceship on the front cover. His spots looked even worse today, like they were about to start oozing white goo.

I gulped and looked quickly over at Jaz. If she looked up and saw me talking to Adam,

14

that would be it. She'd know I really was a loser then. Like I'd been at my old school.

I tried to laugh. "Thanks, but – I don't actually like to read very much."

"You don't?" He looked amazed. "But you like stories, don't you? Films?"

Go *away!* I thought. "Yeah," I said, "but ..."

"Well, a book's just like a film that goes on in your head. And this one's great. It's about these people who get trapped on a spaceship, and ..."

Jaz and her group started heading towards us. They were talking and laughing. They hadn't noticed me yet, but I knew any second now they would. Before Adam could say anything else, I grabbed the book and shoved it in my bag.

"Thanks," I said, not looking at him. "I've got to go to the loo now."

I rushed off before he could reply. *Why did I have to meet him yesterday?* All I needed at my new school was this geeky boy to latch onto me! I had to sort this out right now.

I tried to avoid him for the rest of the day. It wasn't difficult because we didn't have any classes together. Bankside put all the clever, spotty kids together in their own group.

I was in Jaz's group. I watched her as the day went on, and I knew that I'd been right. She was the centre of Year Nine, the hub of everything. I knew I had to be her friend for the others to like me.

But Jaz wasn't interested in me at all. Half of our teachers talked about me at the start of their lessons. They said I was new and told everyone to make me welcome. But Jaz didn't even bother to roll her dark eyes or smirk at her friends.

It was as if I didn't exist.

That night I picked at my dinner and didn't say much. No-one else did either. Gemma was scowling as she looked down at her fish and chips. Mum kept rubbing at her temples as she ate. Her short, streaky blonde hair looked flat and scruffy and not at all like the sleek haircut she'd had a few months ago.

"Um ... how was work?" I asked at last.

Mum looked up. "Hmm? Oh, all right, I guess." She gave a sigh. "I wish I could get something that paid more ..."

Mum had got a job at an insurance company. She used to be a secretary years ago, after Dad died. That was before she and Dan got married. Dan was a banker, and made shed-loads of money. Mum hadn't had to work or worry about money for years. Now everything was different.

A piece of fish flopped onto the floor. "Gemma!" Mum said with a groan. "Try to be more careful."

Gemma shoved her plate away. "I don't like this. It tastes funny."

"Eat it anyway," snapped Mum.

"I want chicken nuggets."

"Well, there aren't any." Mum picked up the fish and put it back on Gemma's plate.

Gemma's face twisted up. "I want my dad! Dad would let me have chicken nuggets."

"Your dad's not here," said Mum firmly.

"I want to ring him ... can't I ring him? Please!"

My heart stopped. I stared at Mum. She wouldn't let Gemma ring, would she? Gemma would tell Dan where we were!

Mum's face had gone pale. She slowly shook her head. "No, Gemma. I told you before why you can't ring Dad. Maybe later we'll fix something up but not now ..."

Gemma let out a sob and ran from the table. Her chair fell over, banging onto the floor. I could hear her crying in our room a few seconds later.

Mum slumped her head down into her hands. I wanted to say something to her, but I couldn't. We wouldn't even be here if it weren't for me.

I stood up and cleared our plates away. *Forget it*, I told myself. *There's nothing you can do about it. Just concentrate on Jaz, on how you can be her friend.*

So that's what I did.

****

At break the next day I saw Jaz. She was leaning against a wall in the courtyard and eating a packet of crisps. I had lain awake for hours the night before and I'd planned what I would say to her. But now I couldn't get my feet to move. It was like I had turned to stone.

In the end, I edged forward a few steps. As I walked up to Jaz I practised what I would say. The line I'd planned was, *Hi, I'm Kylie. What do you do for fun in this stupid school?*

"Look at that," Jaz said loudly. "God, how pathetic."

Oh no! I froze. Was she talking about me? Everyone's head turned to look but they weren't looking at me. I turned to look too. Adam was walking by, reading a book. He was actually *reading a book* while he walked. Thank God he hadn't seen me.

Jaz shook her dark head. "Something should be done about him. He's a bloody show-off. He thinks he's so clever."

"He lives in my block of flats," I said. My cheeks flushed bright red. That wasn't what I'd meant to say. Everyone looked at me. I wanted to shrink, like I always did. But this time I stood up tall, and looked back at them.

"Who are you?" said Jaz as she popped another crisp in her mouth.

I smiled, and tossed my brown hair back like I had seen Jaz do. "Kylie Winters. We've just moved here."

Jaz looked bored already. "Yeah, and ...?"

"And Adam thinks we're friends ... it's really sad."

There was silence for a moment. I thought I'd blown it. Then suddenly Jaz laughed. "Hey, that's great. We could do something with that." And I was in, just like that.

Chapter 3
The Voices in my Head

"Right, tell us everything," said Jaz that day at lunch. I felt like I'd won the lottery. It was only my second day at Bankside, and here I was sitting with the most popular girl in school!

"What do you want to know?" I asked.

She rolled her black eyes. "What he said to you! What you said to him! Come on, Kylie, it's not hard." One or two of the others sniggered. Izzy sniggered the loudest.

I bit my lip, trying frantically to remember. "Well – I was sitting in this allotment next to our block of flats, and Adam came in ..."

Jaz snorted. "What were you doing in the *allotments*?"

I felt my cheeks burning. I wasn't about to tell her how I'd been desperate to see a bit of green. "Just messing about," I said.

"OK, fine. So Adam came in, and then what?" Jaz wanted to know.

"Well, he started talking about science, and this clock he's making ... and how he's really into science fiction, stupid crap like that."

Jaz took a swig of Coke. She didn't look impressed. I tried hard to think of something else. "Oh, and he asked what I was doing there. I told him that the voices in my head had told me to go and talk to him ... he actually seemed to believe it for a second."

Jaz almost spat out her drink. "He didn't! God, he's such a weirdo!"

That was when I got my idea.

I don't know where it came from. It just dropped into my head and it was perfect. And I could tell when I looked over at Jaz that she had come up with the exact same idea.

"It's perfect!" she said softly and her eyes sparkled.

"What, what?" asked Izzy in a high voice.

Jaz nudged me. "Tell her, Kylie."

Jaz Parbinder was asking *me* to tell everyone what was what! I smiled, trying to look as cool and relaxed as Jaz. "It's easy. I'll tell Adam that I really *do* hear voices in my head." I looked quickly over at Jaz. I was suddenly scared that I had got it wrong.

24

"That's right!" she grinned. "Yeah, let him think you're a total psycho. Serve him right, the creep."

"And then, and then—" I almost jumped up and down in my seat as I grabbed Jaz's arm. "We can get him to do things! Like, we'll tell him that the voices in my head will make me hurt myself or something if he doesn't!"

"Ooh! He'll have to *prove* his friendship," crooned Jaz. She winked at me. "Good one, mate."

Mate. I sat back in my chair with a huge smile on my face. All around me the faces were a mix of excitement and envy. Excitement because of what we were going to do to Adam ... and envy because I was Jaz's new friend.

We spent the rest of the day planning together. In between the lessons we swapped ideas and giggled. At last we knew what we were going to make Adam do. And OK, yes, I knew it wasn't very nice ... but it was also *extremely* funny. I hadn't laughed so hard in ages. Not since before Mum married Dan.

"OK, listen," said Jaz. "From now on, we don't know each other at school, right? We'll swap moby numbers and that, but little Adam mustn't guess you're up to anything with me." She gave my arm a squeeze. "Oh, Kylie, this is going to be *ace.* I'm so glad you moved here!"

****

Adam looked surprised when I walked up to chat to him after school that day. "I thought you were hanging out with Jaz Parbinder and that lot," he said.

I shook my head. "No ... they're not very nice, really." Behind me, I could see Jaz and the others. They'd heard what I'd said and were falling over themselves laughing. Jaz gave me a quick thumbs-up behind Adam's back.

Adam looked pleased. "It must be really tough, being in a new school."

"Oh … it's not too bad." I couldn't look at him properly, or I'd burst out laughing. I tried to sound weird, like I was listening to voices that weren't there.

Adam made a face. "Really? I think it's hard enough just going to *school*, never mind a new one."

Yeah, I bet, I thought. *That's because you have no friends.* "No, it's not hard," I said in the same far-away voice. "They tell me what to do." Then I shook my head like I was just coming awake, and tried to look puzzled. "Oh, sorry … what was I saying?"

Adam stared at me. "You said *they* tell you what to do. Who are they?"

I shook my head quickly. "I didn't say that."

"Yes, you did."

"Well, I didn't mean anything by it."

Adam was still frowning at me. I pretended nothing had happened. "Listen, tell me more about this science project you're doing. The thing with the water clock?"

"Oh, yeah, it's really interesting ..." And then he was away. He talked on and on about this machine he had built. How it had taken him over a year, and now he was going to enter it in the Science Fair next week ...

"Kylie, are you listening?" he broke off suddenly. We were almost back at our block of flats by then.

I blinked. "Oh, yeah, sorry ... what were you saying?"

"What's wrong?" Adam was starting to look upset.

"Nothing. It just gets sort of ... noisy in my head sometimes ..." I said.

"*Noisy?* What do you mean?" Adam didn't look upset now. He was looking *scared*.

I had to look away. I thought I might burst out giggling I was feeling so nervous. "I mean it's noisy with all the voices telling me what to do all the time, inside my head. On and on, they never shut up."

"Who's *they?* That's the second time you've said that!"

"*Them.* The voices—" I stopped. "No, I can't tell you. They'd hurt me."

"*Hurt* you? What—" Suddenly Adam grabbed my arm. "Come on, we can't talk here. Let's go to the allotments."

He had a key for the gate on his key chain, so we went in and sat on the bench. Nobody else was around. I drew a pattern with my finger on the wooden bench. God, this was almost too easy! Adam seemed so upset, and I'd hardly even said anything.

"What's wrong?" he asked. "Who's going to hurt you?"

"It's ... really hard to tell you." I gulped and looked down at my feet.

He touched my arm. "But I'd like to help."

"It's just ..." I took a deep breath. "Well – when I met you the other day, I said something about the voices in my head. Remember?"

His eyebrows drew together as he nodded. "Yeah, I remember."

"Well, I said it was a joke, but ... but it's not, really. I hear voices in my head, all the time. Horrible, angry voices, telling me to do things—"

"What things?" whispered Adam. He looked shocked. His eyes were big and round behind his glasses.

"To – to hurt myself." Like Jaz and I had planned, I pulled up the sleeve of my brown school sweatshirt and showed him a big scratch on my arm. I had got it a few days ago at the shelter, just before we left, when I'd fallen against the sharp edge of a table.

Both of us stared down at the scratch. Adam didn't say a word for a long time. Then he said, "Kylie, you've got to tell someone!"

"I am, I'm telling you!" I quickly pulled my sleeve down again. I didn't like looking at the scratch. The truth was, I *had* thought about cutting myself a few times, when we were still living with Dan. I never had, but it still scared me to think about it.

"But you need help!" Adam's voice rose.

"You can't tell anyone!" I grabbed his arm. "Please, Adam, you can't! The voices would make me hurt myself, really, really bad if you did. In fact—" I broke off, and put both my hands up to my head.

"What?" he said.

"They – they're telling me to hurt myself right now. They're telling me that I'm useless, and that I don't have any friends anyway, so why don't I just end it all ..."

All at once, what I was saying felt almost real. My eyes filled up with hot tears and I couldn't say anything else.

Adam's face was so pale that it looked like a glass of milk. "I'll be your friend. Kylie, I really will! Don't hurt yourself again—"

I shook my head. "No ... no, they say you don't really mean it. They say nobody would want to be *my* friend."

"I *do* mean it!" he said loudly.

I wiped my eyes. "Well ... they say if you really, really mean it, then you'll have to prove it. Only – only what they want you to do sounds so stupid! I know you'll never do it, not in a million years. *No*-one would ..."

"I will!" Adam's face was twisted up with worry. "Just tell me what to do!"

So I did. I told him what I wanted him to do. Jaz and I had thought of something that would be a real laugh. For us.

It was as easy as that.

Chapter 4

I am a Haddock

Jaz and I met in the girl's loo the next morning before our first class. "Did you do it?" she asked.

I grinned. "Yeah, it was simple. He believed every word I said." I felt bad as I thought about how upset Adam had been. But it was his own fault that he believed such a stupid story! That's what I told myself, anyway.

"Excellent!" Jaz said and punched the air. "Oh, I am so looking forward to this."

The first bell rang. Jaz winked at me, and went out into the corridor. I waited a few seconds and then went out too. That way, no-one would think we'd been talking together.

Adam was just coming up the front steps. He looked like a tall, skinny scarecrow. I tried to hide. I waited just behind the lockers. Would Adam really do it? I could see Jaz and the others. They were waiting for him in a group by the door.

"Hi, Adam!" called Jaz as he came inside. Her dark eyes were sparkling. "How you doing?"

Adam blinked. I could see he didn't understand why Jaz was being so nice to him. Then he took a deep breath, and I saw him stand up tall. My heart thudded. He really was going to do it!

"I am a haddock," he said to her.

Jaz grinned. The group of people round her fell about laughing. "You're a *what*?"

"I am a haddock," Adam said again. His face was as red as his spots now. "Blub, blub," he added.

Oh my God! Our plan had worked. I felt excited and guilty all at the same time. I pressed my fist up to my mouth so that I wouldn't giggle. Adam saw me then. I tried to look as if I was upset, instead of laughing.

He came over to me. He looked serious now. "Don't worry, Kylie," he whispered. "I'm going to keep saying that. All day long, just like you said. You can tell your voices that. Tell *Them* you've got a friend now."

He walked off down the corridor. I watched him go ... and I didn't really feel like laughing any more.

Jaz and the others came up to me as soon as he'd gone. Jaz gave me a quick hug. She had an enormous smile on her face. "This is brilliant! Oh, I *wish* I could be in the boffin group, just for today!"

I grinned back at her, and told myself to lighten up. He wasn't going to get *hurt* or anything. What's more, I wasn't ever going to go through that bullying crap again. With Jaz as my friend, no-one would touch me.

Adam did what he'd promised. For the rest of the day, when anyone talked to him, he said, "I am a haddock. Blub, blub." By lunchtime it was all over the school that Adam Hughes had gone mental.

"Where are your gills, mate?" shouted a boy as everyone was coming into the canteen for lunch.

"I am a haddock," replied Adam, looking straight ahead.

The boy grinned and pushed into him. "A *what?* A carp? A tuna?"

Adam went on looking straight ahead. Then he said, "I am a haddock. Blub, blub."

Everyone fell about laughing. I could see Jaz and the others. They were holding onto each other, they were laughing so much. Jaz shot me a quick grin.

Then, as Adam was getting his lunch at the counter, one of the teachers passed by and told him to tuck in his shirt.

Adam put down his tray and tucked his shirt in but he didn't say anything. The teacher said, "Well? What do you have to say for yourself?"

I saw Adam lick his lips.

"Speak up!" barked the teacher.

"I am a haddock," mumbled Adam.

The teacher stared at him. "*What* was that, Hughes?"

"I am a haddock," Adam said again. His face was so red it looked like a blazing forest fire. "Blub, blub."

"Very funny!" snapped the teacher. "Half-hour detention this afternoon."

I had got my lunch and was sitting at one of the tables by then. Adam sat down beside me. His face was still fire-engine red, but he gave me a small smile. "How am I doing?"

I could feel Jaz and the others looking at us from across the room. I made myself smile back at him. "Um – thanks. I – I didn't really think you'd do it."

He took a deep gulp of his water. "I told you ... I'm your friend. So those voices will just have to back off, right?"

I bit my lip. I didn't say anything.

Adam's eyes behind his glasses were a light blueish-grey colour. "I mean, it'll be OK after this, right? They'll go away, and not make you hurt yourself any more."

I nodded quickly. "Yeah, I'm sure it'll be OK after this ..."

But, deep down, I knew that Jaz wouldn't just let the game drop. She was having way too much fun.

And to be honest ... so was I.

****

That night at dinner, Mum looked more tired than ever. There were dark rings under her eyes, and I could tell that she had a million things on her mind. Even so, she tried to smile at me.

"How was school? Are you making new friends?"

I looked up. Mum actually seemed to want to know, for a change. She'd always wanted to know about my life before we had to move, but that seemed so long ago now.

I nodded. I felt good she was asking me to tell her. "Yeah, there's this girl called Jaz. Everyone likes her, and—"

The phone rang and I had to stop talking. Mum stood up to get it. "Hello?"

"I hate *my* new school," said Gemma. She looked down at her plate with a frown.

"*Hello?*" I could hear Mum say again. I could see her eyes flicker with panic as she waited for a reply. Suddenly she hung up the phone and sat down again.

"Who was that?" I asked.

She shook her head quickly. "Nobody. Just a prank call ... what were you saying about school?"

Gemma went very still. "Was it Dad?"

My stomach twisted. Oh, God, it *couldn't* have been Dan, could it? He didn't know where we were! I stared at Mum. I hoped so hard that she would say, *No, of course not, don't be silly.*

She slowly shook her head. "I ... I don't know," she said. "We've had a few odd calls, but I don't know how he could have got our number—"

"I want to talk to Dad!" broke in Gemma. Her eyes filled up with tears. "It's not *my* fault we had to go. Why shouldn't *I* get to talk to him?"

"Because you can't," said Mum. Her voice was low and worn out. "And I've said before, it's no-one's fault. You know that. It was just what we had to do."

She didn't sound like she meant it. She didn't even look at me.

I started to shake. I pushed my chair back and stood up. "I'm not hungry any more … can I go and do my homework?"

That night I lay awake and looked up at the ceiling as Gemma snored and snuffled in her bed across the room from me. Was I the only one who was glad that we had left? Gemma was too young to know anything. Anyway, Dan had always treated her as if she was a spoiled little princess.

But what about Mum? *She must be glad to have got away from Dan*, I thought. Things had been so awful! There had been so many times when I had gone downstairs and found her crying …

Beep. My mobile had a new text. I rolled over in my bed and picked up my phone.

MEET ME IN GIRLS LOO AGAIN 1ST THING 2MORROW. WE HAVE 2 PLAN WHAT 2 DO 2 ADAM NEXT!!!

43

Chapter 5
More Proof

"The voices want more," I said to Adam at morning break. "They want more proof."

Adam looked worried. "*More* proof? What do they want now?"

I thought about what Jaz and I had planned that morning. It had seemed really funny at the time, but ...

Get on with it, I told myself. There was no way I could back out now. Jaz would never be my friend again. I took a deep breath. "They ... they said that it was too easy, what you did before. That you weren't really in any danger. So it wasn't like you were proving anything."

For a second, Adam didn't look as if he believed me. "They want me to be in *danger*?"

I put both my hands up to my head again, as if I was hearing loud voices. "Stop it!" I muttered. "Be quiet! I can't ask him to do that, I can't ..."

Adam grabbed my arm. "Kylie! What are they saying?"

I made sure that there weren't any teachers around. Then I put my hand slowly down into my bag. "The voices want me to show you this," I whispered. I pulled out the razor that Jaz had given me that morning. I held it flat in my hand.

All of the blood drained from Adam's face. "What – Kylie, what—" he said.

"It's what *They* make me use to hurt myself," I said. "They – they make me carry it around all the time." I couldn't look at him as I put the razor back in my bag. I knew Jaz and the others were hidden somewhere and watching us, probably wetting themselves laughing.

Adam looked shocked. "Oh, God! Kylie, give it to me, OK? Tell them I'll prove I'm your friend, but you have to give me that razor!"

"You'll really help?" I said.

He nodded. "Just give me the razor!"

I handed it to him, and he shoved it in his bag. "Don't hurt yourself again, OK? Promise me!"

He really looked scared. I felt awful suddenly. God, what were we *doing*?

Then a picture of Dan flashed into my mind. I remembered how he stank of whisky, how he shouted at me and pushed at me with his hand. *You stupid, useless cow!* he'd said *No-one likes you, do they? Do they?* Something in me went hard, as if everything was Adam's fault.

"No, I can't promise that," I said. "You need to prove that you're my friend before I can promise."

And I told him what he had to do.

******

Paul Patterson was in Year Nine like the rest of us, but he *shaved* already. You could tell from the dark stubble on his chin. He was massive, with thick arms like a gorilla. He walked through the corridors with long, swinging steps and he would scowl at everyone around him. Jaz said Paul Patterson was definitely not someone you wanted to mess with. I think I would have worked that out on my own, even if she hadn't told me.

Paul was very, very surprised when Adam picked a fight with him after school that afternoon.

"Hey Patterson, get out of my way." Adam pushed Paul from behind as everyone was going down the front steps.

Paul's face was dark and angry when he turned around. "What's up with you, you geek?"

My stomach churned with a sort of deep excitement as I watched. Jaz and the others stood in a group a few metres away at the bottom of the steps. They nudged each other, their eyes gleaming. Jaz gave me a quick wink.

Adam stood up tall. "I – I told you to get out of my way, that's all. So move!" He gave Paul another push.

Other people had stopped to look now. A crowd began to gather. "Fight, fight," chanted someone.

Paul looked *puzzled* more than anything else. He stared at Adam like Adam had escaped from the loony bin. "Have you gone flippin' mental?"

Adam blinked, then said again, "You heard me! MOVE!" He pushed into Paul's chest, and Paul stumbled backwards so that he almost fell.

That was when Paul lost his temper. He roared like a lion as he grabbed at Adam. He tackled him in the stomach, and they both crashed onto the steps. Suddenly there were fists flying everywhere. You could hear Paul hitting Adam.

"Fight, fight!" screamed the crowd. The school doors flew open and Mr Munro, the PE teacher, ran out. He yanked Paul off of Adam and held him back as he kept trying to punch Adam again.

"Patterson, not you again!" he shouted.

"It wasn't him, sir, it was Adam!" yelled someone. "He kept pushing Paul and telling him to move!"

Adam stood there looking stunned. Blood ran from his nose in a bright red stream.

"Adam?" Mr Munro turned and looked at him. "Is this true?"

"Yes, sir," muttered Adam. He wiped at the blood on his face and then he turned and saw me. He looked miserable. His glasses had been knocked off, and one of his eye-lids was starting to swell up.

I stared down at the ground. I felt as if I might throw up.

Mr Munro grabbed hold of both boys and took them inside. As the crowd started to drift away, Jaz ran over to me, her dark eyes shining. "Kylie, that was fantastic! That stuck-up creep is really getting what he deserves. Blimey, he doesn't know what's hit him! No, hang on, yeah he does – *Paul* hit him!"

Everyone fell about laughing. Izzy was actually clutching her sides.

"Listen, I don't want to do this any more," I blurted out. "It was funny at first, but – but enough's enough, right?"

"Wha-at?" Jaz stared at me. "We can't stop *now.* It's just getting good."

"But I didn't know we'd actually hurt him!"

Jaz rolled her huge eyes. "Well, what did you *think* would happen if you made him pick a fight with Paul, you thickie?"

"Yeah, but ... " I didn't say anything else. Yeah, I guess I had known ... but I hadn't *known,* not really, not until I saw Adam with blood streaming down his face.

"There's no way we're stopping now," said Jaz flatly. Her face looked hard. "You'll *do* it, right?" she said.

She didn't add *Or else you know what will happen*, but I could hear the words hanging in the air just as if she had said them. I looked at Izzy, and saw an eager leer on her face. I knew she was hoping like mad that I'd say no. Then they could make *me* the next target.

I gulped and nodded. "I'll do it one more time, and that's all. Then – then I'll tell him that the voices have gone away. OK?"

Jaz glared at me. Then she gave a long, slow smile. "Perfect. One more time, a last proof of his friendship."

I licked my lips. "I won't tell him to pick a fight again, or – or anything like that."

Jaz hooked her arm through mine and gave me a squeeze. She smiled sweetly. "Oh, don't worry, we'll think of something else for Adam-boy to do. But if it's the last time, then it better be a good one … right?"

Chapter 6
Talking Back

I walked home slowly. *How did I get myself into this mess?* I was thinking. Maybe Adam wasn't someone I wanted to be friends with, but it still wasn't right to treat him like this. And more than that ... I was starting to feel scared. I thought about how excited I'd felt when Adam pushed into Paul, and a shudder ran down my spine.

One more time, I told myself. *Then it will all be over with.*

Mum was waiting for me when I got back to our flat. As soon as I saw her, I knew I was in trouble.

"Kylie, where *were* you?" Her face was like a thunderstorm. "You know I depend on you to get home on time to look after Gemma! Haven't I got enough to worry about? You promised me you'd be here. That way I can get Gemma from school and then go back to work afterwards."

It felt like she had slapped me. "I'm sorry, I—"

She grabbed up her jacket. "I don't have time to talk about it now. I have to get back to work." The door banged shut behind her as she left. Her footsteps hurried down the stairs.

"Ooh, you're in trouble," smirked Gemma.

"Shut up," I snapped. "It's nothing to do with you."

She made a face at me, turned on the TV and flopped down on the floor to watch. I sat on the brown, saggy sofa and glared at the screen. It was one of those stupid kids' programmes, with dancing puppets everywhere. I was just about to tell her to switch channels when the phone rang.

I picked it up. "Hello?"

"'Zat you, Kylie?" I heard someone say.

I froze. Oh, God, no. It couldn't be.

"Answer me!" my stepfather shouted. "I can hear you breathing ... know you're there. Lemme talk to Jane."

Jane was my mum. I gulped. "She's – she's not here."

"You're lying! Put 'er on the phone."

My heart was thudding so hard I thought it might explode. "I can't, I told you. She's not here."

Gemma had stopped watching TV. She was staring at me. I tried desperately to look as if I wasn't talking to anyone important.

I heard ice clink in a glass as Dan took another drink. "Listen, you," he hissed, "put your mother on the phone or you'll be sorry. This is all your fault! You listen now ..."

"What d'you mean?" I whispered.

"Yeah, she'd never have left me if it weren't for *you*, always talking back, making trouble! I'd still have a happy marriage! But she'll never make it on her own, will she? She likes the good life too much."

He laughed. It felt like a rusty saw cutting through me. "Yeah, I'll find out where you are and get her back, you'll see. All I'll have to do is act sweet and say sorry, and *then* you'll see, you little—"

I hung up quickly. Then I took the phone off the hook and shoved it under a sofa cushion.

"Who was that?" asked Gemma. She was still staring at me.

"No-one!" My voice sounded odd and far away. Oh God, was what he'd said true? Would Mum really go *back* to him? She hated her life now, I knew she did. What if he *did* find us, like he said? It would be even worse than before!

"Gemma, I've got to go out for a while," I said.

"But you're supposed to be baby-sitting me!" She looked scared.

"I won't be long – I've just got to get out of here—" I grabbed my jacket and raced out the door.

Once I got outside, I didn't know where to go. I sank down onto the front steps, hugging myself and trying not to cry. *How* had he got our number? And if he had *that*, it wouldn't take him long to find us ...

"Kylie?" said a voice.

I looked up. I hadn't heard anyone come up to me. Adam was standing there, without his glasses. I guess he'd just got home from school. His face looked awful, all red and sore.

He put his bag down and sat beside me. "Kylie, what's wrong?"

"Where are your glasses?" I asked. His face looked odd without them.

He shrugged. "They got broken ... I can see without them, sort of."

Guilt rushed through me. "Are you in lots of trouble?"

"Not too bad. The headmaster was sort of in shock. I mean, just yesterday I was telling him about my water clock. We were talking

59

about entering it in the Science Fair next week, then today I'm dragged into his office for fighting. He couldn't work out what was going on."

And it was all because of me. I couldn't say anything.

"It's just lucky he said they wouldn't ring my mum this time. I mean—" Adam bit his lip. "Um ... listen, Kylie, is everything OK now? You look upset."

I didn't want to tell him, but somehow it came out. "No, it's my stepfather. He – he just rang ..." A huge lump choked up my throat, and I couldn't finish.

Adam just watched me, and waited for me to keep talking.

I looked down. "He's ... really awful. He married Mum when I was only four, and I know I'm meant to love him, but—"

"Sometimes that's impossible," said Adam. He sounded bitter.

I took a deep breath. "He drinks … and he shouts at me. He says awful things. Sometimes I think he really hates me, only I don't know what it is I've done! He seems to like my little sister OK, but then she's *his* kid, and I'm not …" Tears welled up, and I looked away.

Adam stared down at his hands. "Does he hit you?" he asked softly. "My dad did that too."

It felt like a cold breeze had swept over me. I shivered as I began to remember Dan again. *Don't you talk back to me, you little cow!* he'd said. *I'll teach you not to talk back to me!*

"You don't have to tell me," said Adam.

"He never used to hit me," I said slowly. "But then one time when he was shouting at me, I couldn't take it any more. I told him he was a stupid drunk, and why should I listen to anything he said? And ... he sort of went berserk."

Adam moved closer to me and took my hand. I hardly even noticed. I wiped my face. "Um – he started hitting me, over and over, and I fell ... I guess he knocked me out. Mum came home and found me lying on the floor, and took me to hospital ... she told them I fell down the stairs. But then a few days later, when Dan was away on a business trip, she packed all our things and we left. He mustn't find out where we are now."

"Wow." Adam stared at me. "Your mum sounds really brave."

"I guess ..." I watched the cars driving past. "But Adam, she blames me for it, I know she does!"

"*Blames* you? Because your stepdad beat you up?"

I nodded. "She thinks it's all my fault ... she always used to tell me that I shouldn't say anything to make him angry. And then I did, and we had to go – and now she *hates* it here. I'm so scared that he'll find us, and she'll go back to him!"

Adam squeezed my hand. "You need to talk to her, Kylie. I bet it's not like you think."

I stared at the ground. "Maybe."

There was a long silence. Adam let go of my hand. "Um, Kylie ... do you think that the voices in your head have anything to do with your stepdad?"

"What do you mean?" I asked. For some reason my heart started pounding.

Adam blushed. Then he went on, "Well, you said that your stepdad doesn't like you, and says terrible things to you ... and, well,

They do the same thing, don't they? It's like you've got your stepdad inside your head."

It was such a horrible thought that I couldn't say anything. Adam tried to smile. "Ignore me, I'm probably talking crap. But have the voices gone now?"

I looked at Adam's spotty face and his blue-grey eyes, and I wanted so much to tell him yes. But then I thought of Jaz, and what she and her friends could do to me. I was filled with cold fear. I shook my head.

"They're – they're getting weaker," I said and I hated myself as I went on. "They're starting to think that you're really my friend. But they want you to do one more thing. Just one more thing, and then they'll go away forever."

Chapter 7

Smash Up

When I got back upstairs, my little sister looked like she had hardly moved at all while I was gone. "Was that Dad who rang?" she asked.

I started to lie to her, and then I nodded. "Yeah, and he was really drunk. That's why I had to get out for a bit. It was awful."

Gemma looked at me. "Was he being nasty to you again?"

Nasty. That was one word for it. I let out a sigh. "Yeah."

"Is it – is it my fault?"

I stared at her. "*Your* fault? Why would it be?"

"Because I rang him!" she cried. "I rang him days ago – I only wanted to talk to him—"

"Gemma!" I grabbed her. "You didn't tell him where we are, did you? It's really important!"

"No! I promised Mum I wouldn't, and I *haven't*." She sniffed, and wiped her eyes. "Anyway, he – he wasn't even home. So I just left a message on the answerphone to say I missed him. Then we started getting those funny phone calls ..."

1471, I thought.

I turned to Gemma. "He must have dialled 1471. That's the number you dial on your phone to know the telephone number of someone who's just rung *you*. Dan must have done that to find out our number."

Suddenly Gemma turned and hugged me. I was so amazed that I just stood there for a second, and then I hugged her back.

"I didn't like it when he was nasty to you." Her voice was quiet. "I – I guess ringing him wasn't such a good idea. I won't do it again. And I won't tell Mum you left me on my own."

"Thanks," I said softly, and stroked her hair. Maybe she wasn't such a spoiled brat after all.

Before Mum got home, I put the phone back on the hook. It didn't ring again. So Mum didn't need to know.

****

The next morning I lay in bed, warm and safe under my duvet. I didn't want to go to school that day. I didn't want to see what Adam was going to do. But I had to. Jaz and

the others were waiting for me. They'd know
I'd ducked out of it if I stayed at home.

I walked slowly to school, dragging my
feet. When I got there, I couldn't see Adam
anywhere, and for a moment I was really
happy. Maybe he hadn't come! Maybe he'd
changed his mind!

But then I saw him coming in at the school
gates. He was carrying a large cardboard box,
and he looked pale and grim.

He was going to do it.

Jaz looked at me and smiled. Something
dark danced behind her eyes. She could
hardly wait. I looked away. I felt as if
someone had kicked me in the stomach. I
knew I was no better than Jaz. I wasn't going
to stop him.

Adam walked up to the school steps. My
heart thudded, and I hid behind a gang of
Year Tens. He was going to do it *now*, just

like I'd told him. And oh, God, I didn't want him to see me! I didn't want him to look at me. Not while Jaz and the others were sneering at him.

Adam put the box down softly on the ground and stepped back from it. "Attention!" he yelled. "Your attention, please!"

Everyone stopped talking and stared at him. "Hey, it's Haddock Face!" yelled someone.

Adam's face turned red. It looked like his spots were on fire. But his voice was firm as he kept talking. "I've made a water clock for the Science Fair," he said. "I've ... been working really hard on it." He nudged the box with his foot.

My jaw dropped open. He hadn't brought *that*, had he? That stupid clock he kept on about! I had only told him to bring something important to him, not *the* most important thing. What had he done? What had *we* done?

"So what, you geek?" shouted a boy in my year group.

Adam swallowed. "So ... this."

I couldn't bear it any more. I jumped out from behind the gang of Year Tens, but before I could shout *No!* Adam had lifted his foot and then kicked the box. There was a sound of cracking wood and smashing glass. He stamped on it again, and again, until the box was almost flat.

No-one moved or said anything. Adam stood there and stared down at the wreckage.

"Look at him, he's a total nutter," whispered someone.

Suddenly the sound of laughter floated on the air. Jaz. She walked forward, her face bright with delight. Her cronies followed on her heels. They were all laughing as if the sight of Adam and his broken box was the funniest thing they had ever seen.

"Right, well *I've* got something to say too now," cried Jaz. "And here it is ... all of this was a *set-up*, you loser! And you fell for it!" She grabbed Izzy's arm and the two of them nearly fell over, they were laughing so hard.

Adam stared at her. He didn't move. His face had gone as white as a ghost's.

"It was all Kylie!" Jaz said. She pointed at me. She was talking to the crowd now and laughing so much she could hardly get the words out. "She – she told him that she heard these voices called *Them* and that *They* would make her hurt herself if he didn't do things for her ... *I am a haddock, I am a haddock!*"

Everyone stared as Jaz walked over to me. She put an arm around me. "Well done, Kylie! You're a brilliant actress!"

No-one said a word. Then slowly some people started to laugh. The laughter grew louder and louder, until everyone had joined in. In the middle of it all, Adam just ... stood there. Not saying a word.

Stop laughing, it's not funny! I wanted to scream. I couldn't get the words out. It felt like my feet had become roots and were dug into the ground. Adam turned and looked at me and at Jaz ... and his face grew hard as he took in the utter guilt on my face. Without saying anything, he scooped up his broken box and walked off, out of the school.

Chapter 8

Edward

The bell rang, and everyone started to head inside. Jaz still had her arm around me and she squeezed me tight as we went in. "Kylie, that was brilliant. How did you get him to stamp on his stupid clock? God, I wouldn't have missed that for ..."

Something hot and angry exploded inside of me. I shoved her away. "Shut up!" I shouted. "Just shut up!"

Jaz looked back to see if there were any teachers around, then she pushed me into the girls' loo. Izzy followed right behind.

"What's up with you?" Jaz wanted to know.

Warm, salty tears started to pour down my face. "I didn't know you were going to – to *announce* it to everyone like that!"

Jaz looked shocked. "But that was the idea, wasn't it? To get back at him for being so stuck up!"

"No! I mean … I mean, I don't know." I looked away and wiped my eyes with my hand.

Jaz put her hands on her hips. "For God's sake, Kylie! It was all your idea in the first place!"

My chin snapped up. "It was not! It was *both* of us—"

"No, you're the one who thought of making him do things," put in Izzy. She couldn't hide her smirk of delight. "It was all *your* idea, and now you're acting all goody-goody."

Jaz shook her head and sneered. "I thought you were OK, Kylie, but I was wrong. You're as geeky as *haddock-boy,* aren't you?"

"Yeah, with a *face* like a haddock, too," crowed Izzy. She was loving this, you could tell.

The second bell rang. It echoed through the girls' loo, and Jaz and Izzy left. Jaz gave me a look as she went out of the door that told me I'd be *haddock-girl* for ever so far as she was concerned.

I would never be in her group now. Never.

I didn't care any more. I propped myself up against the sinks and stared into the mirror. I remembered Adam's face as he had looked at me.

What had I done?

Suddenly I pushed away from the sinks and walked out of the school. The school secretary was busy with a parent who was asking her about something. Even if she'd noticed me, I'd have walked out. The main doors swung shut behind me, and I ran down the steps.

Cars whizzed past me as I walked slowly down the street. I knew without thinking about it where I was going. And sure enough, Adam was there, digging in the ground like he was trying to stab it to death with every push of his garden fork.

"Hi," I said, not sure what to do. I stayed by the gate of the allotments.

Adam glared at me. "Come to tell me about some more voices, have you?" His voice shook. "What's the problem now, eh? Are they telling you to go throw yourself off the roof or something, unless I smash something *else* of mine?"

Next to him on the ground, I could see what was left of his clock. It was totally flattened. Gone forever.

"I'm sorry," I whispered, as I went on staring at it.

Yeah? Well, not sorry enough." He turned back to his digging. He jammed the fork into the ground with his foot. His school trousers had dirt all over them.

"I still want to be your friend," I said. I don't know where the words came from, but I knew they were true the moment I said them. Adam ignored me.

"Adam?" I took a step forward. I wished that he'd look at me.

He threw the fork down with a clatter. His face was red, near tears. "Just piss off, Kylie! Go back to Jaz and have a good laugh, why don't you!" He stopped. He didn't even look at me. "Better yet, go jump off that roof that *them* are telling you about."

I backed off. I was shaking, and I turned and ran home. I couldn't face going back to school again, not now.

Our flat felt empty and silent. I sat on the sofa and stared out of the window. I had to make it up to him, somehow! But the problem was ... there was nothing I could do now. His clock was gone. I couldn't bring it back. And I couldn't take back the sound of everyone laughing at him after he'd smashed it.

He had done it to *help* me. The thought made more tears start running down my cheeks. Stupid tears! They weren't going to make anything better. I wiped them away.

I was still sitting there when Mum got home with Gemma. She stopped short in the doorway and stared at me. "Kylie! You're back early. Is something wrong?"

Gemma ran past me into our bedroom. She was singing to herself. My mouth felt dry. I licked my lips, and blurted out, "Yeah. Dan rang yesterday."

A look of shock passed across Mum's face. I hadn't meant to say that, hadn't meant to tell her. But now I had to. I took a deep breath, and told her every word of the phone call.

She pressed her fist up to her mouth. "How did he get our number, *how*?"

I shrugged. There was no use getting Gemma into trouble. Mum let out a breath, and sank down beside me on the sofa.

"Does – does that mean he can find us?" I could hardly get the words out.

Mum said softly. "I don't know. I hope not."

"Is it true, what he said?" My hands were tight fists. "Will you go back to him?"

Her chin jerked up. "No! Of course not!"

"But he said that all he had to do was say sorry, and—"

"Oh, Kylie ... how could you think I would *ever*—" Mum stopped. Her eyes filled with tears. "After coming home and finding you like that, and seeing what he'd done to you ..."

I swallowed hard. "Then – then you don't blame me for having to leave him?"

A look of deep sadness touched Mum's face. She shook her head. "No. No, Kylie. I blame myself, for staying with him for so long."

Could she really mean what she was saying? "But you seem so unhappy here! I thought ..." I said.

Mum touched my hair. She stroked it with her hand. "I'm sorry. It's been a hard time for me. I've had to go back to work again and take care of the three of us ... but I'm doing it. He can ring all he likes. He can even turn up here and say whatever he wants, if he tracks us down. But we're still never going back to him, Kylie. That's a promise."

I leaned up against her and closed my eyes. She put her arms around me, and we held each other for a long time. Suddenly I said, "I was bullied at my old school."

Mum sat up. She looked upset. "Kylie! Why didn't you tell me?"

"I guess I was embarrassed." I stared down at the sofa, my face going red.

She rubbed my arm. "Well ... is everything OK now? Has changing schools helped?"

I didn't answer at once. After a bit, I said, "Sure. Everything's fine."

After about ten more minutes, Mum went back to work. Gemma came out of her bedroom and turned on the TV. I sat and watched her stupid shows with her. But I wasn't really watching them at all. I had too much to think about.

Adam was right. Mum was really brave. She was making a new life for us. Going back to work to keep things going. I was such a coward next to her! I couldn't even stand up to a bunch of schoolgirls.

Suddenly everything felt different. I felt strong and brave for once. I sat up, grim and ready to fight back. I *wasn't* going to be a coward. I'd show Adam how sorry I was for what I'd done.

I knew what I had to do. It was awful ... I didn't want to do it. But it was the only thing that might work.

****

Adam didn't come back to school the next day, or even the day after that. It took two days for him to walk back into school and when he did, he didn't look at anyone. He didn't say a word. But plenty of people talked to him. They punched him on the back and laughed. "Hey, haddock! Made any more clocks while you were away?" Ha, ha.

He didn't talk to any of them. He avoided me most of all. I tried to get him to notice me a few times during the day, when I saw him between classes. I'd been hoping that he had forgiven me, somehow, and that I wouldn't have to do what I'd planned to make up for how awful I'd been to him.

Jaz and Izzy and the others had been ignoring me the last few days. They turned away any time I came near them. Izzy had hissed *haddock-girl* at me a few times, but that was all. Because Jaz was who she was, the rest of our form ignored me too. It was as if I had some sort of awful disease that they could catch if they so much as looked at me.

83

And I knew they were about to think I was *really* odd. I was scared. Could I go through with my plan?

When lunch came around, I waited for the teachers in the queue to get their food and go off to the staff room. Then I climbed up on a chair at the back of the canteen. I knew the canteen staff wouldn't do anything. They only get involved if there's a riot.

"Hey, everyone! Look at me!" I cried. My voice came out as a strangled squeak. No-one noticed me.

"LOOK OVER HERE!" I called again, louder this time. That did it. People started nudging each other and whispering. Some of them got up and walked over to me. They began to grin. Jaz stared at me with narrow eyes.

Across the canteen, Adam had looked up from the table where he was sitting by himself. He watched me. He was frowning.

"Um ... I want to make a public apology," I said. My face felt like it was on fire. "You all know what for, right? I just wanted to get in with Jaz. I wanted to be her friend and for her to like me, because – well, because I was stupid. I acted like a jerk, and I lost a good friend because of it."

I looked Adam in the eyes, my face burning. "Adam, I'm sorry."

He didn't say anything. I heard Jaz laugh, but no-one joined in, for a change. A sea of serious faces looked up at me.

I swallowed hard. I was trying not to cry. "But saying 'sorry' isn't enough, and I know that. That's why ... that's why I brought this." I reached into my bag and pulled out Edward, my old teddy. A couple of people sniggered.

I felt clammy and sick. *Oh God, I don't want to do this!* I thought. But I had to. It was the only thing I could do.

I held onto Edward. "I – this is – this is a teddy bear my dad gave me. It's the only thing I have from him ... My dad's dead. That means Edward's sort of like Adam's clock was for him. Something really, really important."

Without looking at anyone, I bent down and took a pair of scissors out of my bag. I heard a gasp as suddenly everyone knew what I was going to do.

"What a *loser*," I heard Jaz mutter. The rest of the crowd just went on staring at me. They couldn't take their eyes off Edward.

Holding him up by one paw, I opened the scissors and moved them towards his neck. My mouth was trembling, but my arm was steady. I snipped the scissors open and shut around Edward's neck and began to cut. One of his seams popped. Another one. Tears started to run down my face, but I kept cutting.

"No!" shouted a voice. Adam jumped up. He pushed people aside. "Kylie, stop it!" He got to my chair and grabbed at my arm. Then he pulled Edward away.

"Stop it," he said. I saw his glasses had been repaired and his face wasn't so red and swollen. His blue-grey eyes stared firmly into mine.

"I have to do this!" I choked out. "Because of what I did to you ... your clock ..."

"Well, this won't make it come back! Come on, get down." Adam took the scissors off me and helped me off the chair.

Someone began to clap. Then all at once the rest of the crowd started. A few people were whooping and cheering. I stared around me and blinked. People were smiling at me. At both of us.

"Well done, Adam!" shouted someone.

"That took a lot of guts," I heard someone else say.

I saw Jaz looking round her. Her face was cold and cross. She and Izzy glared at me, but I hardly noticed.

"Come on, leave the two love-birds alone!" shouted someone. The crowd drifted away back to their tables until Adam and I stood by ourselves at the end of the canteen.

I was so embarrassed I couldn't speak. I hugged Edward. His neck had a deep cut in it, with bits of fluffy white stuffing poking out.

Adam was blushing. He touched the cut gently. "Can you fix him, maybe?"

I nodded and wiped my nose with my hand. I was still crying a bit. "Yeah, I – I guess I could try sewing him."

Adam took a deep breath. "Kylie, that was really ... that was really a stupid thing to do. A really, really stupid thing."

"I wanted to do it," I said. "I knew I could never say 'sorry' enough ... I had to show you."

A slow smile grew across his face. "Yeah, well. It was still really stupid of you."

I started smiling, too. We stood there like a pair of idiots, not talking, just smiling away at each other. In the end, Adam said, "Come on, lunch is almost over ... let's sit down and eat."

I nodded. "OK. But Adam, listen – I'm really not into science, you know. Or reading, or ... well, anything that you're into, probably."

Adam waited for a moment, then he grinned. "That's OK," he said. "I'm not really into teddy bears. We can still be friends, can't we?"

A warm, happy feeling swelled up inside of me, like sunshine. "Yes," I said. "We definitely can."

Barrington Stoke would like to thank all its readers for commenting on the manuscript before publication and in particular:

L. Alder

Kavita Anand

Aileen Chafer

Becky Clack

Grace Copperwhite

Charlotte Davis

Aisha Douglas

Amy Ertan

Francis Harkin

Michaela Ireland

Juliette Kelly

Riona Kelly

Starr Lee

Declan Lindsay

Chloe Morris

Nicky Mustoe

Helen Oates

Emma O'Nien

Mrs Eva Philips

Jordan Piper

Emily Rennebach

Ellen Roberts

Amber Stokes

Jordan Tandy

Shazia Saddiq

Cecily Skeggs

Aislin Smyth

Carol-Anne Stangham

Robyn Stock

Emily Wright

Become a Consultant!

Would you like to give us feedback on our titles before they are published? Contact us at the email address below – we'd love to hear from you!

info@barringtonstoke.co.uk
www.barringtonstoke.co.uk

More exciting titles!

Crow Girl

by Kate Cann

ISBN 1-842993-46-1

Lily is an outsider. Girls bully her, boys don't know she's alive. She begins to hide from her troubles at the nearby Wakeless Woods. But she is not alone. The crows are there. Watching. When she finds the crows, she finds herself – and a burning need to show everyone at school the *new* Lily.

Will this Halloween be a night to remember?

You can order *Crow Girl* directly from our website at **www.barringtonstoke.co.uk**

More exciting titles!

Text Game

by Kate Cann

ISBN 1-842991-48-5

Everything's great in Mel's life. And the best bit's Ben. He's gorgeous, he's fun and great to be with – she can't believe he's going out with her. Then she starts getting nasty text messages. They say Ben's going to dump her. They say he's seeing someone else. Are they just from some jealous nutcase, like her friend Lisa says? Or are they telling the truth?

You can order *Text Game* directly from our website at **www.barringtonstoke.co.uk**

More exciting titles!

Cold Keep

by James Lovegrove

ISBN 1-842993-63-1

The sun sets on the icy wastelands of Cold Keep, and Yana faces the greatest danger of her life. The Shadow Trolls are hunting. And Yana must fight them alone. She will come back a hero ... if she comes back at all.

One warrior. A million shadows. Who's hunting who?

You can order *Cold Keep* directly from our website at **www.barringtonstoke.co.uk**